IT'S A WONDERFUL LIFE

Published by World Publications Group, Inc.
140 Laurel Street
East Bridgewater, MA 02333
www.wrldpub.com

Reprinted 2011 by World Publications Group, Inc.
Copyright ©2006

ISBN-13: 978-1-57215-458-2
ISBN-10: 1-57215-458-6

Printed and bound in China by Toppan Leefung
Printing Limited.

1 2 3 4 5   06 05 03

Page 1: Donna Reed and Jimmy Stewart as
Mary and George Bailey in Frank Capra's *It's a
Wonderful Life.*

Page 2: Having discovered that he really did have a
wonderful life, George is reunited with his family.

It's a Wonderful Life

Cast

George Bailey....................James Stewart
Mary Hatch........ ....Donna Reed
Mr. Potter.............. ....Lionel Barrymore
Uncle Billy...................Thomas Mitchell
Mrs. Bailey........................Beulah Bondi
Ernie....................................Frank Faylen
Bert...Ward Bond
Clarence............................Henry Travers
Mr. Gower..........................H.B. Warner
Violet............................Gloria Grahame
Harry Bailey...........................Todd Karns
Ruth Daken.....................Virginia Patton
Pa Bailey........................Samuel S. Hinds
Nick.............................Sheldon Leonard

Director-Producer Frank Capra

Screenplay............................Frank Capra,
Frances Goodrich,
and Albert Hackett

Additional Scenes Jo Swerling

Based on a story by
Philip Van Doren Stern

INTRODUCTION

Regarded by many as *the* Christmas movie, Frank Capra's *It's a Wonderful Life* is a sentimental favorite starring Jimmy Stewart as George Bailey, a would-be suicide who is saved by an angel named Clarence, played by Henry Travers. Clarence, who hopes to earn his wings by proving to George that life is indeed precious, shows him what life would be like if he had never existed.

Stewart was nominated for an Oscar for his performance as George, the dutiful son who always wanted to leave his small hometown to see the world but instead stayed home to preside over the family-owned Building and Loan.

Left: One of Hollywood's favorite leading men, Jimmy Stewart played numerous characters epitomizing honesty and decency and other American small town values.
Above: Stewart played the title role in *The Glenn Miller Story* (1953).

The part of George Bailey was the sort of role at which Jimmy Stewart excelled. With his slow drawl and gangly walk, Stewart was something of an oddity among leading men, but it was this unique style that made him a star.

Stewart arrived in Hollywood in 1935 and played a few bit parts until Frank Capra discovered that the awkward country boy manner was perfect for *You Can't Take it With You* (1938) and *Mr. Smith Goes to Washington* (1939). W.S. Van Dyke also made the most of Stewart's charm in *It's*

Left: Although she usually played the all-American girl, this still from *Ransom* (1956) highlights the glamorous side of Donna Reed.
Below: Early in his career Jimmy Stewart appeared in *Seventh Heaven* (1937).

a Wonderful World (1939). Jimmy Stewart received the New York Film Critics award for Best Actor for these three films, and in 1940 he won an Academy Award for *The Philadelphia Story*. In a roundabout way, Stewart attributed his Oscar to Frank Capra, believing that if he had not received rave reviews for *Mr. Smith Goes to Washington,* he never would have been cast in *The Philadelphia Story.*

It's a Wonderful Life was Stewart's first movie after World War II. In the films that followed, Stewart's film persona matured, and he was cast in a variety of roles—detectives, heroes, athletes, and other rugged individuals. He reprised the quiet, absent-minded sort in *Harvey* (1950) and was again nominated for an Academy Award. One of America's favorite movie stars, Jimmy Stewart continued to play leading roles well into the 1970s.

Donna Reed played Stewart's wholesome and devoted wife in *It's a Wonderful Life*. A farm girl from Iowa, Donna Reed began her career as Donna Adams, playing bit parts in minor films for MGM. By the mid-1940s, she was an established leading lady, almost always cast, as she was in *It's a Wonderful Life,* as a sincere and wholesome character.

Her one departure from this mode was the part of Alma, the prostitute in *From Here to Eternity* (1953). Although Reed won an Academy Award for Best Supporting Actress for her performance as Alma, her film career was beginning to wane and she made a successful transition to television as the star of her own long-running series, *The Donna Reed Show.*

Lionel Barrymore, one of Hollywood's finest actors, played the perfect villain—Henry F. Potter, "the meanest and richest man in the county." The rest of the supporting cast included Gloria Grahame, Thomas Mitchell, Samuel S. Hinds, Beulah Bondi, Ward Bond, and Frank Faylen.

It's a Wonderful Life was based on a story called *The Greatest Gift* by Philip Van Doren Stern. Unable to have it published, he sent it to his friends as a Christmas card. RKO Studios heard about the story, bought the rights to it, and commissioned

Right: The part of Clarence Odbody, Angel Second Class, was delightfully played by Henry Travers.

three different writers—Dalton Trumbo, Marc Connelly, and Clifford Odets—to each develop a script. When Capra heard the story, he knew it would make a wonderful film. However, he felt that none of the three scripts did justice to the original story and hired Albert Hackett and Frances Goodrich, a husband and wife screenwriting team, to write another script. Capra himself collaborated with them on the new script.

The theme of *It's a Wonderful Life* is typical of the films directed by Frank Capra. As in *It Happened One Night* (1934), *Mr. Deeds Goes to Town* (1936), and *You Can't Take it With You* (1938), *It's a Wonderful Life* underscores the belief that humanity is basically good and that good will triumph over evil.

One of the directors who helped shape the Golden Age of Hollywood, Capra was a champion of the little man. His hallmark was light, romantic movies with upstanding characters. However, when *It's a Wonderful Life* was released in December 1946, the mood of the nation was changing and postwar audiences found Capra's film to be naïve and sentimental. Reviews were mixed—some critics declared it a masterpiece; others found it filled with "Pollyanna platitudes." Capra, however, didn't care what the critics thought. He thought it was the greatest film he had ever made. In fact, he thought it was the greatest film anybody ever made—a sentiment that is shared by millions of movie lovers.

Left: This still of Donna Reed and Jimmy Stewart was one of many taken by RKO's publicity department to create the image of a happy, loving relationship between George and Mary.

Frank Capra's first and only choice for the role of George Bailey was Jimmy Stewart. Stewart had just been discharged from the service and hadn't appeared in a film in close to six years, and was eager but anxious about making another film. As Capra recalled in his autobiography, he invited Stewart over to listen to a story idea. Halfway through the telling Capra jumped to his feet, declaring, "I haven't got a story. This is the lousiest piece of cheese I ever heard of. Forget it, Jimmy... Forget it!" But Stewart didn't forget it. He was eager to work with Capra again and repeat the success of *You Can't Take it With You* (1938) and *Mr. Smith Goes to Washington* (1939).

George Bailey was the sort of role at which Jimmy Stewart excelled—the all-American boy next door, nice but somewhat gawky. Stewart's characters are generally regarded as filled with goodwill, but his portrayals were sincere, never maudlin, and underneath the surface was a complex persona. George Bailey, for example, was an upstanding citizen, but when he feels oppressed by the pressures of daily life he contemplates suicide.

A native of Indiana, Pennsylvania, Jimmy Stewart began his acting career in a Boy Scout production. After graduating from Princeton with a degree in architecture, he joined the famed University Players, where he met Henry Fonda and Margaret Sullavan. After Stewart arrived in Hollywood, Sullavan helped his career by insisting that he be cast in her films.

Though he didn't have the classic good looks and smooth manners of the typical leading man, Jimmy Stewart had a special charm that quickly won the hearts of audiences all over America. Stewart excelled at romantic comedy and won an Academy Award for his performance as the journalist who falls in love with Katherine Hepburn in *The Philadelphia Story* (1940).

When World War II broke out, he enlisted, serving as a bomber pilot. He achieved the rank of a full colonel and remained in the Air Force Reserve, retiring as a brigadier general in 1968.

After the war, Stewart expanded his repertoire, with a variety of roles, giving one of his most memorable performances as Elwood P. Dowd, the mild mannered tippler, in *Harvey* (1950), which earned him his fourth Academy Award nomination. He was nominated for a fifth Academy Award for his performance in Otto Preminger's *Anatomy of a Murder* (1959). He also appeared in westerns, and was a favorite of director Alfred Hitchcock. Stewart made only a few films in the 1970s and retired from acting in the late 1980s. Jimmy Stewart died on July 2, 1997.

It's a Wonderful Life is set in Bedford Falls, an imaginary small town somewhere in New York state. It is Christmas Eve, and the first thing we hear as the movie begins is the sound of voices praying for George Bailey.

This is George Bailey's crucial night. George is despondent and contemplating suicide. The angels must send someone down to save George, but the only angel available is Clarence Odbody, Angel Second Class. Sweet, but inept, Clarence has yet to earn his wings and become a full-fledged angel. Before he heads down to earth, however, the heavenly powers fill him—and the audience—in on George's life.

The action begins in the year 1919, when George Bailey is 12 years old. George and a group of friends are sliding down an icy hill onto a frozen river below. When George's younger brother slides down the hill and falls through the ice, George forms a human chain and rescues his brother from the freezing water. George's heroics cost him the hearing in his left ear. This early scene reveals a great deal about George's character. We learn that George thinks of others first, even to the extent of endangering his own life.

This scene foreshadows the romance between George Bailey and Mary Hatch. Here we see a young Mary Hatch (Jean Gale) order a sundae from George Bailey at Gower's drugstore. When he turns away from her, she whispers that she will love him forever. This scene reveals George's urge to see the world, as he explains the virtues of coconut to Mary.

While fixing the sundae for Mary Hatch, George discovers a telegram to Mr. Gower informing him of the death of his son. Distraught over this tragic news, Mr. Gower has mistakenly filled a prescription with cyanide. George is supposed to deliver the fatal prescription. An obedient and diligent boy, George must do his job, but if he follows Mr. Gower's orders, someone may die.

When George returns to the store still holding the poison pills, Mr. Gower begins slapping him for disobeying him. The scene ends in a tearful embrace, with George vowing he would never tell anyone about Mr. Gower's mistake.

Later, when Clarence shows George what the world would be like had he not intervened, we learn that Mr. Gower's error proved fatal and he was sent to prison and became an alcoholic.

The part of Mr. Gower was played by H.B. Warner, a distinguished actor of the stage and screen. After starring as Jesus Christ in Cecil B. DeMille's *The King of Kings* (1927), he was typecast in noble, dignified roles and was said to have welcomed the departure from type when given the chance to play Gower as a broken down drunk. Warner was nominated for Best Supporting Actor for his performance as Chang in *Lost Horizon* (1937), another Frank Capra film.

In typical Capra fashion, we have an appeal to home town values. A boy can always count on his dad, and when George (Bobbie Anderson) is confronted with the dilemma of the poison pills, he runs to his dad for help. Though Capra's approach may seem straightforward, his technique was actually quite complex. He had a very clear vision of what a scene should look like. We see exactly what he wants us to see. When George leaves the drugstore, Capra focuses our attention on a billboard with the words: "Ask dad—he knows."

However, George's father, Peter Bailey, is busy with Mr. Potter, so Uncle Billy (Thomas Mitchell) tries to prevent George from interrupting his dad. Note the strings that Uncle Billy had tied around his fingers. Unfortunately, they do little to improve Billy's poor memory, and his absentmindedness will be a source of much anguish for George in the future.

Peter Bailey (Samuel Hinds) confronts his arch nemesis—Henry F. Potter (Lionel Barrymore), "the richest and meanest man in the county." This scene established Potter as the villain and Peter Bailey as a man of principle and a defender of the little man. Though he has been almost beaten down by Potter, we can tell that he is prepared to continue the struggle. When George comes to his father's defense, we sense that George will continue his father's fight against Potter and prove a more able adversary.

The part of Henry Potter was played by Lionel Barrymore, who had worked with Capra previously in *You Can't Take it With You* (1938). Capra considered numerous other actors for the part of Potter, but ultimately, decided no one else would do. Indeed, it is impossible to imagine anyone else in the part, so perfectly was it portrayed by Lionel Barrymore. In his autobiography, Capra sang Barrymore's praises: "In any actor's Hall of Fame, Lionel Barrymore's name deserves top billing among the immortals. Yet he was the humblest, most cooperative actor I have ever known."

Lionel Barrymore began his screen career with Biograph in 1909, though he continued to appear on Broadway until 1925. A year later, he signed with MGM, an association that lasted the duration of his career. All told, Barrymore appeared in some 250 films and won an Academy Award for his performance in *A Free Soul* (1931). After two decades as a leading man, he moved to character roles in later life and continued to dominate many a film with his strong presence.

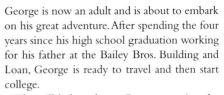

George is now an adult and is about to embark on his great adventure. After spending the four years since his high school graduation working for his father at the Bailey Bros. Building and Loan, George is ready to travel and then start college.

The still below shows George meeting the infamous Mr. Potter. Off screen, their relationship was far from adversarial. Stewart was nervous, having just returned to Hollywood after serving in the war, and Barrymore provided a dose of encouragement.

The throne-like wheelchair Mr. Potter uses is not just a prop. Partially paralyzed by arthritis in the late 1930s, Barrymore did not allow his disability to interfere with his career.

Full of high hopes for the future, an exuberant George heads home (*left*), courtesy of his good friend, Ernie the taxi driver. George's other close friend is Bert the cop, and it seems likely that these two names were inspiration for the *Sesame Street* characters of Bert and Ernie.

Dinner at the Bailey home on the night of Harry's high school graduation. Harry will take George's place at the Building and Loan, and George will go to college. Peter Bailey would like George to return to the Building and Loan after college, but George has a grander vision and declares, "I couldn't face being cooped up for the rest of my life in a shabby little office... I want to do something big, something important." Realizing that his words may belittle his father's life work, he tells him he is a great guy.

This is the last we will see of Peter Bailey, but his influence will continue to be felt. When Potter attempts to close the Building and Loan, George will continue his father's work and champion the rights of the common man.

For the role of Peter Bailey, Frank Capra chose Samuel S. Hinds, a character whose demeanor was suited to the roles he typically played—the wise and dignified older gentleman. Years later, Frank Capra described Samuel Hinds to a film class: "He looks like a father. He's so perfect he looks like two fathers."

Stewart wondered whether he should age as the film progressed. Capra said that he would handle the details of George's aging process. Physically, nothing was done to Jimmy Stewart's appearance to create the effect that George Bailey was growing older. But it is a credit to Stewart's acting ability and to Capra's direction that the audience accepts that Stewart, who was then 38, was in his early 20s and filled with a youthful enthusiasm.

At the graduation party, George encounters Mary Hatch (Donna Reed), seeing her for the first time since she was a young girl. Much to the chagrin of Freddie, the young man she had been talking to, Mary only has eyes for George. Freddie was played by Alfalfa Switzer of the *Our Gang* comedy series.

For the part of Mary Hatch, Frank Capra originally wanted Jean Arthur. However, she had a previous commitment on Broadway, and Capra was forced to continue his search. Olivia DeHavilland, Martha Scott and, according to the Hollywood rumor mills of the day, Ginger Rogers were also considered for the role. In the end, Capra went to MGM and found Donna Reed.

Donna Reed made her film debut in 1941 in *The Getaway*. For the rest of the decade she played roles similar to Mary Hatch—the wholesome, pretty girl next door. Although she played that type of role to perfection, it was her one departure from the type, the prostitute in *From Here to Eternity* (1953), that earned her an Academy Award for Best Supporting Actress.

In 1959, she returned to television and the long-running series *The Donna Reed Show*, in which she portrayed the perfect wife and mother. In the mid-1980s, she replaced the ailing Barbara Bel Geddes in the television series, *Dallas*. Donna Reed died in 1986.

These pages: At the party George and Mary enter a Charleston contest, but unbeknownst to them, Freddie, Mary's jealous suitor, is plotting his revenge. The dance floor is situated above a pool and a simple turn of the key will expose the pool. Carried away while dancing, George and Mary don't see the floor disappearing beneath them, and fall into the pool. Soon, everyone has jumped into the pool, including the school principal.

Capra received several letters expressing doubt about the believability of this scene, but the pool was real (the scene was filmed on location at Beverly Hills High School), and the scene was based on an actual event.

Pages 32-33: Wearing borrowed clothes to replace their pool-soaked party wear, George walks Mary home as they sing "Buffalo Gals."

Below: On the way home, George and Mary pause in front of the old Granville place. "It's full of romance, that old place. I'd like to live in it," Mary tells George, as he hurls a rock through a window and makes a wish to see the world. Mary interrupts George's reverie with a wish of her own.

When George starts to kiss her, Mary runs away, loses her robe and jumps into the hydrangea bushes (*left*). George's good-natured teasing about Mary's unusual predicament is interrupted by tragic news—his father has suffered a stroke.

In this scene Frank Capra pits good against evil as Potter attempts to shut down the Building and Loan following Peter Bailey's death. George Bailey pleads his case for keeping the Building and Loan open, and while Potter concedes that Peter Bailey was a "man of high ideals," he maintains that Bailey was a poor businessman and the Building and Loan is a losing proposition.

If Potter has his way, Peter Bailey's worst fears would be realized. Potter would become the only source for borrowing money, and the decent, hard working people of Bedford Falls would be denied their piece of the American Dream.

George has given up his long-cherished dream of traveling in order to handle affairs at the Building and Loan in the months after his father's death. He is due to leave for college as the board of directors gathers to vote on the future of the Building and Loan.

When Potter bemoans the "starry-eyed dreamers who stir up the rabble and fill their heads with a lot of impossible ideas," George comes to the defense of his father and the townspeople: "Just remember this, Mr. Potter. This rabble you're talking about. They do most of the working and praying and living and dying in this community! Well, is it too much to have them work and pray and live and die in a couple of decent rooms and a bath?"

The board agrees to keep the Building and Loan operating under one condition—George remains in charge. "This is my last chance," cries George, but he sacrifices his personal dreams and sends his younger brother Harry to college in his place.

To numerous filmgoers, *It's a Wonderful Life* epitomizes the films of Frank Capra, whose populist message embraced the triumph of the common man over the system. In the Capraesque world, honesty and decency challenge deceit and selfishness—and win.

A Sicilian immigrant, Frank Capra was a real life rags-to-riches success story. He spent his youth working his way through school alongside the common man who would figure so prominently in his films. Capra's films applauded the home grown virtues of the working class and made him a favorite with depression-era audiences. During the 1930s, he won three Academy Awards for Best Director in five years: *It Happened One Night* (1934), *Mr. Deeds Goes to Town* (1936), and *You Can't Take it With You* (1938). By the decade's end, Capra was considered one of the preeminent directors of his generation and became one of the first directors to earn the honor of having his name featured above the title of a film.

When the United States entered World War II, Capra joined the Signal Corps and made 11 *Why We Fight* documentaries used for indoctrinating the troops. His work in support of the war effort earned him the Legion of Merit and the Distinguished Service Medal. After the war, Capra teamed with fellow directors William Wyler and George Stevens and production head Samuel Briskin to form Liberty Films with RKO. The first movie he made for Liberty Films was *It's a Wonderful Life*.

Frank Capra made only five films after *It's a Wonderful Life*, none of which equaled his earlier successes. *It's a Wonderful Life* would remain his favorite film, and he would show it in his home every Christmas Eve.

George has bided his time at the Building and Loan for four years while his younger brother Harry (Todd Karns) was attending college. Eagerly clutching brochures about faraway places, George waits at the train station for his brother to return from college. With Harry at the helm of the Building and Loan, George can at last leave Bedford Falls. But once again George's hopes and dreams go unfulfilled, for Harry is accompanied by his new bride (Virginia Patton) and has plans to work for his father-in-law in Buffalo. George, as we might expect, stays in Bedford Falls and manages the Building and Loan.

The conversation recedes into the background as Capra directs our attention to the face of George Bailey. In an instant, George has correctly assessed the situation. There's a look of despair on George's face, and it's a look we've seen before and will see again. We first saw George's desperation when the board made him executive secretary of the Building and Loan, and then again when George hears a train leaving Bedford Falls, its whistle a symbol of lost hopes and dreams.

One of the elements that made Capra's films so successful is that he effectively represented real life desperation. *It's a Wonderful Life* is the triumph of the common man, but it is also the triumph of the spirit.

Left: A publicity still of George, Mrs. Bailey (Beulah Bondi), and Uncle Billy (Thomas Mitchell). Beulah Bondi was well-suited for the part of George Bailey's mother. All told, she appeared as Stewart's screen mother seven times.

Above: A successful character actor, Thomas Mitchell began his career as a reporter for the Elizabeth, New Jersey, *Daily Journal*. He then tried his hand at writing plays and acting, moving from the stage to the screen in the mid-1930s. In 1939, he won an Academy Award for Best Supporting Actor for his performance as Doc Boone in John Ford's *Stage Coach*. That same year he also appeared in two of his most memorable films: *Only Angels Have Wings* and *Gone with the Wind*. An actor known for his diversity, Mitchell continued to make films the rest of his life. He made his final screen appearance in another Frank Capra film, *A Pocket Full of Miracles* (1961), which was also the director's final film.

After leaving the party celebrating his brother's marriage, George encounters the town flirt, Violet (Gloria Grahame). She has always had her eye on George, but his proposition for the evening is not quite what she had in mind. He tells her, "Let's go out in the fields and take off our shoes and walk through the grass. Then we can go up to the falls. It's beautiful up there in the moonlight. There's a green pool up there... and we can swim in it, and then we can climb Mt. Bedford and watch the sun rise against the peaks..."

Violet thinks George is crazy, and the townspeople who have gathered around them are amused by George's wild ideas. This scene offers Violet as a counterpoint to Mary Hatch. While George is obviously attracted to Violet, she is not the right woman for him because she does not understand the romantic, dreamy side of him. In contrast, Mary listened eagerly to George and his wild ideas when he spoke of lassoing the moon. In fact, she has carried the memory of that night with her for the last four years, as we shall see on the following page.

"George Lassos the Moon"—Resigned to staying in Bedford Falls, George leaves the party for Harry and wanders through Bedford Falls. After his walk through town, George ends up at the home of Mary Hatch, who has just finished college. Remembering the night four years earlier, when he promised her the moon, she has drawn a portrait of him lassoing the moon.

George and Mary stand close to each other, listening to Sam Wainwright on the phone offering George "the chance of a lifetime" in his new business. George is very much aware of the nearness of Mary and can no longer deny that he loves her, but it is an admission that does not come easily. Having always been consumed by the desire to see the world, George does not want to admit that he can be happy in Bedford Falls.

Mary is the antithesis of George. She has no desire to leave Bedford Falls, and in fact had been eager to return to her hometown after finishing college and working in New York.

Mary represents the best of Bedford Falls—she is small town goodness, optimism, and best of all, love. She is what keeps George in Bedford Falls and makes him happy.

Jimmy Stewart was nervous about this scene because it was his first screen kiss since his return to Hollywood after the war. Perhaps Stewart's own case of nerves contributed to George Bailey's feverish urgency. Under Capra's watchful eye, Stewart filmed the scene in only one take, and it worked so well that part of the embrace was cut because it was too passionate to pass the censors.

Top: George and Mary are married, and George is finally about to embark on his long-wished for trip, with Mary at his side.

Bottom: It's raining on George and Mary's wedding day, and though the weather is dreary the newlyweds are naturally happy as they celebrate their marriage until Ernie the taxi driver notices the townspeople running toward the bank. A bank run threatens the financial institutions of Bedford Falls, including the Building and Loan. As Mary and George head to the train station to leave on their honeymoon, the camera zooms in on them, watching as the worried citizens of Bedford Falls race to the bank and to the Building and Loan to withdraw all their funds.

Pages 50-51: George steps from the cab as Mary pleads with him not to stop. Once again, George cannot leave his family and friends in a time of crisis. He races in the pouring rain to the Building and Loan and finds that Uncle Billy has locked the doors, creating more panic among the people.

Capra did a little extra research and discovered that it was raining in New York state the day of the bank run of 1933. To add veracity to the scene, he decided to have it rain in Bedford Falls for the bank run scene.

George unlocks the doors and allows the anxious citizens to charge into the Building and Loan. Uncle Billy is nervously taking a wee nip to calm his nerves. "This is a pickle, George. This is a pickle," Uncle Billy says with much agitation. The bank has called in their loan, leaving them with no cash on hand—and a mob of worried townspeople who want their money now!

On the counter is Jimmy the Raven, a regular in every Frank Capra film since *You Can't Take it With You* in 1938. When he wasn't assigned a part in *It's a Wonderful Life*, Jimmy took matters into his own hands—or wings—and flew onto the set. Capra promptly wrote Jimmy into the script.

Meanwhile, Potter is waiting, like a vulture circling a body. In a meeting with the president of the bank, he has seized control of the bank, closing it down for a week, and is plotting to do the same with the Bailey Bros. Building and Loan. Ready to prey on other people's misfortunes, he is counting on panic taking over and is offering the Building and Loan shareholders only 50 cents on the dollar for their money. This is a prime opportunity to run the Building and Loan out of business once and for all.

Though Barrymore's performance as the greedy villain was flawless, Capra called on the makeup department to provide a little extra assistance. Since Barrymore had appeared in a number of films as a loveable curmudgeon, Capra wanted to alter Barrymore's appearance slightly so that there would be no positive associations with his previous roles. Wearing a plastic cap to modify the shape of his head, Barrymore was transformed into the skinflint everyone loves to hate.

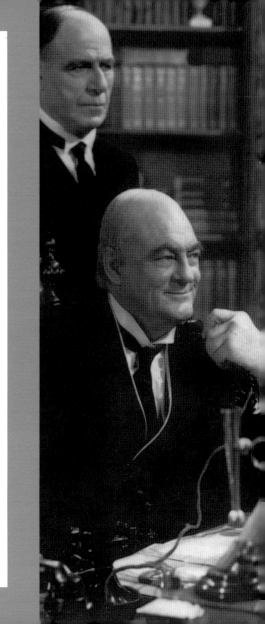

George and Uncle Billy face the worried crowds. In contrast to the overwrought Uncle Billy, George Bailey is a study of grace under pressure.

The bank run sequence highlighted Jimmy Stewart at his best. Capra needed an actor who could be idealistic and compelling, whose passionate beliefs could give him the power to sway a crowd. As he explained in his autobiography, Capra believed "films were novels filled with living people. I cast actors that I believed could be those living people. James Stewart was Jefferson Smith [in *Mr. Smith Goes to Washington*] and George Bailey." How right he was.

Right: Uncle Billy, Mary, and Ernie the taxi driver listen as George tries to allay fears of the people.

The part of Ernie the cab driver was played by Frank Faylen, a character actor with numerous films to his credit. A versatile actor, his roles ranged from the amiable cab driver in *It's a Wonderful Life* to the sadistic male nurse in *The Lost Weekend* (1945). Television fans remember him as the father of Dobie Gillis on *The Many Loves of Dobie Gillis*. He later was featured on *That Girl*.

Pages 60-61: Mary comes forward with the money that belongs to her and George. This scene allows Capra to demonstrate the goodness of the common man. George appeals to the crowd, asking them to understand that they are all in this together, that their money is an investment in the homes of their neighbors. Without the Building and Loan, he tells them, they would all be at the mercy of Potter, who cares naught for the well-being of the people of Bedford Falls.

George's appeal has had the desired effect. Though still scared, the townspeople trust George and most of them agree to withdraw only the money that they need to last the week until the bank reopens.

The third woman in line meekly asked for $17.50—a response that took Jimmy Stewart completely by surprise. He spontaneously leaned over the counter and kissed the woman on the cheek. The exchange worked so beautifully on film that Capra kept it. Though Capra kept tight control of the script and had a clear vision of what he wanted, he was open to an on-the-set inspiration, such as the kiss over the counter.

By closing time, only two dollars remain but the Building and Loan has survived another crisis. George, Uncle Billy, Cousin Eustace (Charles Williams), and Cousin Tilly (Mary Treen) congratulate themselves on their financial wizardry and joyfully prance around the room.

One of the hallmarks of Capra's directing style was his attention to detail. He made copious notes on the scripts, adding or deleting material when necessary. Equal care was given to selecting the characters, from the stars to the bit players. Capra's technique for selecting bit players was to forego a screen test and just interview them. "Casting is completely by hunch," Capra remarked in a seminar on directing. "In other words I have to see the man not as an actor but see him as part of the story I'm telling. If I think that's the man, something tells me that's the man, that's the man, and I couldn't tell you why. And he may be not too good an actor, but I don't particularly care because there are no bad actors. There are only bad directors."

Right: "Welcome home, Mr. Bailey." Meanwhile, Mary is waiting for George at their new home—the old Granville place, where she had planned a romantic candle-light dinner, despite the leaky ceiling and crumbling plaster. Outside, Ernie the cab driver and Bert the policeman serenade the honeymooners.

As they embrace, Mary confesses, "Remember the night we broke the windows in this old house? This is what I wished for."

Though the scene is emotional, Capra keeps it from getting overly sentimental by injecting a little humor. When Bert is standing in the pouring rain hanging up travel posters to give the place a touch of romance, his assistant asks, "What are they—ducks?" Then when Bert and Ernie have finished their song, Ernie kisses Bert on the forehead.

Above: Prior to the movie's release in December 1946, this still was seen in lobbies across the United States promoting Frank Capra's *It's a Wonderful Life.*

George never does leave Bedford Falls. Instead, he builds Bailey Park—"dozens of the prettiest little houses you ever saw." Drawing on his personal life, Frank Capra gives us a picture of an Italian family moving into their own home, capping the scene with a nice little speech by George and Mary, as George gives the Martini family a few symbols of happiness and prosperity:

"Bread—that this house may never know hunger; Salt—that life may always have flavor; Wine—that joy and prosperity may rein forever."

But all is not happy with George, as he contrasts his life with that of Sam Wainwright, who has stopped by on his way to a vacation in sunny Florida. Flush with success from his plastic business, Sam rides away in his chauffeur-driven car. Capra focuses on George for a moment. We see the dejection subtly at first as Stewart pauses and stuffs his hands in his pockets and then powerfully, as he kicks the door of his old jalopy.

The audience understands George completely. He is one of us, always struggling and never seeming to get ahead. Potter, shrewd and conniving man that he is, understands George, too. Much to George's disbelief (*left*), he offers him a job at the princely sum of $20,000 a year. Potter's offer seems too good to be true. It represents a fine home, fancy clothes for Mary, and vacations to Europe. George is shocked and asks for 24 hours to think it over.

In this beautifully directed segment, we watch as George comes to his senses (*pages 70-71*). The little gestures that Stewart fills the scene with are simply magnificent. First, he drops his cigar. Then, as he shakes hands with Potter, the horror of what he was contemplating hits him with full force. Stewart looks down at the hand he is grasping—the symbol of everything he has fought against—pulls his hand away, stares at it in disbelief and then slowly wipes it off on his clothing. Do business with Potter—NEVER! How could he have even considered it?

After George's meeting with Potter, Capra uses a narrative segment to advance the plot, as Joseph the Angel brings Clarence up to the present day. George struggled daily at the Building and Loan, fighting Potter all the way. Mary and George had a little boy and girl and then two more children.

Joseph's words paint a portrait of Bedford Falls during World War II. Mr. Gower and Uncle Billy sold war bonds. Ernie the taxi driver, Bert the cop, and Harry Bailey went off to war. George stayed home on account of his bad ear and fought the battle of Bedford Falls, acting as air raid warden and spearheading the paper and rubber drives. While George worked at the Building and Loan, Mary cared for the children, toiled at making the old Granville place a home, and managed the USO.

The publicity still (*right*) of Donna Reed at the sewing machine captures the wholesome image that Capra was after: the devoted wife and mother.

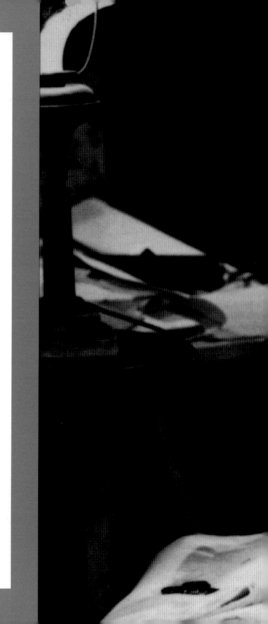

Left: Excitement is building in Bedford Falls. It's Christmas Eve, and one of the town's native sons, Harry Bailey, is a war hero. Harry is calling from Washington, where the president has just awarded him the Congressional Medal of Honor.

This publicity still shows George talking with Harry. By his side are Cousin Eustace and Cousin Tilly. The disgruntled gentleman in the background is Mr. Carter, the bank examiner. This promotional still is slightly different from the scene as it takes place in the actual movie. In the movie, George is wearing his coat and hat, and Mr. Carter is farther away.

Below: The part of Cousin Tilly was played by Mary Treen, a character actress who began her career as a dancer in revues and stage musicals. In the mid-1930s, she started appearing in films, often providing comic relief. As she did in *It's a Wonderful Life*, Mary Treen typically played the part of the working girl.

Right: "I'm glad I know you, George Bailey." George plays Good Samaritan when Violet (Gloria Grahame) asks for money to start her life over in New York.

Above: Frank Capra went to MGM to look for someone to play the village flirt. He had envisioned a sultry blonde sexpot, and as soon as he saw a screen test of Gloria Grahame, he knew he had found Violet.

It's a Wonderful Life gave Gloria Grahame's career a well-deserved boost, but Grahame didn't come into her own until the 1950s. Her seductive voice, pouty lips, and inviting looks made her the perfect choice for the "bad girl." She won an Academy Award for Best Supporting Actress in 1952 for her portrayal of the tramp in *The Bad and the Beautiful* and was absolutely delightful as Ado Annie, the girl who can't say no, in *Oklahoma* (1955). Grahame made only one film in the 1960s, but returned to the screen more often in the 1970s. She died in 1981.

George's happiness turns to heartbreak when Uncle Billy confesses he has lost the money he was supposed to deposit in the bank. While talking to Potter about Harry's bravery in the war, Uncle Billy puts the money, which is wrapped in a newspaper, right in Potter's hand. Potter, of course, sees this as his chance to run the Baileys out of business and keeps the $8,000 for himself. As Uncle Billy says, "Not every heel was in Germany and Japan."

Hatless and coatless, George races through the snow, retracing Uncle Billy's steps. George has reached his breaking point and loses his temper with Uncle Billy (*left*). "Do you realize what this means," he shouts. "It means bankruptcy and scandal and prison. That's what it means. One of us is going to jail. Well, it's not going to be me!"

In this scene, Jimmy Stewart gives a carefully crafted performance of a man totally disheartened. George has just left Uncle Billy. He has given up all hope of ever finding the money, and is on the verge of giving up completely.

Everything Stewart does in this scene contributes to an emotional portrait of despair. Tearfully clutching his son to his chest, he is oblivious to the chatter of his wife and children. When he can shut them out no longer, the tinny repetition of his daughter practicing the piano becomes more than his shattered nerves can take. He screams at her, and four concerned faces turn to look at him in disbelief. Their reaction is equally telling. From their shocked expressions, we can tell that George's behavior is in sharp contrast to his typical persona of loving husband and devoted father.

"Dad, how do you spell frankincense?"

"I don't know," George shouts. "Ask your mother."

At his wit's end, George has no time to help his son, Pete, with his homework. As Mary slowly spells F-R-A-N-K-I-N for her son, she begins to understand that something is seriously wrong with George.

This is a glimpse of the Donna Reed that television audiences would come to know and love on *The Donna Reed Show*. The perfect wife and mother, she was always there to solve a family crisis. In *It's a Wonderful Life*, Mary will take the situation into her own hands and turn to the people of Bedford Falls for help.

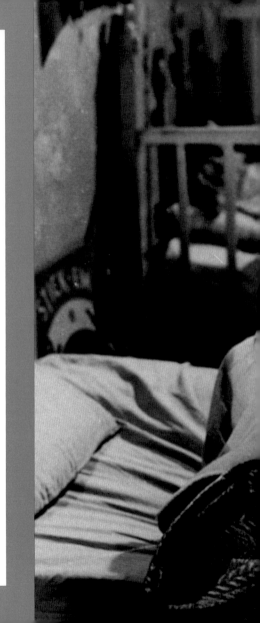

Right: George's youngest daughter, Zuzu, is sick. She caught a cold walking home with her coat unbuttoned so she could protect the rose she won in school. When the petals fall off her flower, she hands them to George to paste back on. Unable to perform such a feat, he turns his back to her, pretending to be fixing the flower, and then sticks the petals in his pocket.

George wanders back downstairs just as Mrs. Welch, Zuzu's teacher, is calling to check on Zuzu. He grabs the phone and yells at her, blaming her for Zuzu's illness. Though his tirade is directed at her, he is really railing at the world.

Below: In his despair, all that George truly values seems a burden. "This drafty old barn! Might as well be living in a refrigerator! Why did we have to live here in the first place and stay around this measly, crummy old town? ...Why did we have to have all these kids?"

Left: George goes to Potter for help, who of course refuses to lend any assistance. Discouraged, he heads to Martini's, a warm, friendly Italian restaurant and bar. The camera moves closer to George, who is seated at the bar. It is clear that he has had too much to drink. He begins to pray, while Nick the bartender casts a worried look in his direction.

"Why do you drink so much, my friend?" asks a concerned Mr. Martini. "Please go home, Mr. Bailey. This is Christmas Eve."

Below: The part of Nick the bartender was played by Sheldon Leonard. In later years a hugely successful television producer, Leonard began his career as a stage actor before turning to the screen. Sheldon Leonard died in 1997.

Right: Seated at the bar near George is Mr. Welsh, the husband of Zuzu's teacher. His wife cried for an hour after George lashed out at her, so Mr. Welsh feels justified in popping George a good one. "That's what you get for praying," mumbles George as he wanders drunkenly out into the snow.

After leaving Martini's, George crashes his car into a tree. Leaving his car behind him, he crosses a bridge and is about to jump into the icy water. Now is the time for Clarence (Henry Travers) to make his entrance, which he does rather dramatically, suddenly falling from above into the swirling water beneath George. Without a moment's hesitation, George jumps in to save Clarence.

Once the two of them are out of the water Clarence explains to George that he is his guardian angel (*pages 90-91*), and that he has just saved George's life. George is slightly taken aback, thinking he was the one who had just rescued Clarence, but Clarence calmly explains his logic: "I knew if I were drowning, you would try to save me." And Clarence was right—George always thought of the other person.

George doesn't quite know what to make of this odd fellow in the funny underwear. Clarence goes on to explain that he is the answer to George's prayers. He is here to save George and earn his wings in the process.

"...I wish I had never been born," George tells Clarence. With Joseph's help, Clarence grants George's wish. The snow stops, the howling wind blows the door open—and George Bailey doesn't exist. He has no worries or obligations. No one knows him. He can hear out of his bad ear; his lip has stopped bleeding; ~~and~~ his clothes are dry. Gone are his car, his driver's license, and Zuzu's petals.

Henry Travers brought warmth and understated humor to the part of Clarence Odbody, AS2 (Angel Second Class). Travers was a veteran of the British stage before he moved to Broadway in the 1920s and then Hollywood in the 1930s. A highly regarded character actor, Travers starred in a number of films including *Dark Victory* (1939), *High Sierra* (1940), *The Bells of St. Mary's* (1945), and *The Yearling* (1946), He won an Academy Award for Best Supporting Actor for his performance in *Mrs. Miniver* (1942).

Previous pages and right: George and Clarence trudge over to Martini's for a drink. The once convivial place is now a smoky, sleazy joint, and there's no Mr. Martini. Nick, now a surly character, owns the joint. As Clarence chatters away happily, Mr. Gower stumbles in, a drunkard since he went to prison for his fatal mistake with the poison capsules.

"Look, who are you?" George asks Clarence after they've been tossed out of the bar.
"I told you, George. I'm your guardian angel."
"Yeah, yeah..."
"You've been given a great gift, George. The chance to see what the world would be like without you."

George discovers that the world is indeed a very different place without him. Bedford Falls is Pottersville. Filled with dive bars, nightclubs, and pool halls, all its small town charm is lost. There is no Building and Loan. Violet is a cheap floozy, Mary is an old maid, George's mother runs a boarding house, Uncle Billy is in an insane asylum, and his brother Harry died in that sledding accident because George wasn't there to save him.

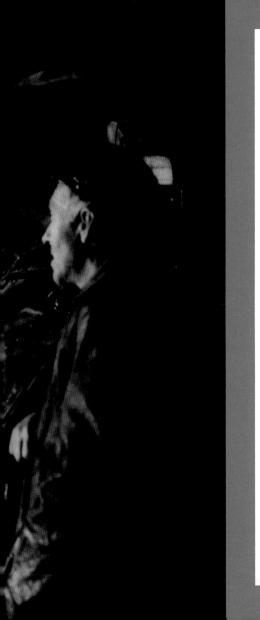

George's best friends, Ernie and Bert, don't know him, and his house is empty, deserted for twenty years. Of course, George has no children because he himself was never born.

One of the most effective techniques of the unborn sequence is each actor's subtle change in appearance. As Mrs. Bailey, Beulah Bondi, has an aura of warmth and understanding, but once her character becomes Ma Bailey, the proprietress of a boarding house, her face is hardened and suspicious. Ernie's (Frank Faylen) friendly demeanor is replaced with hostility. H.B. Warner takes Gower from a respectable, white-collared druggist to a bum suffering from D.T.s his face covered with stubble. Sheldon Leonard's Nick, once the concerned bartender, has become belligerent, and Donna Reed's Mary—the picture of fresh-faced beauty—is transformed into the stereotypical old maid. Where she once had a lighthearted spring to her step, her walk is now stiff and guarded.

"Strange, isn't it? Each man's life touches so many other lives, and when he isn't around, he leaves an awful hole, doesn't he?"

Slowly, George realizes that Clarence is right. The final blow is seeing Mary—plain, wary, and completely devoid of the joy of the life that once illuminated her personality. When George can no longer take the ugly reality of life in Pottersville, he flees from the center of town, gunshots ringing in his ears. Clinging to the bridge where he jumped in to save Clarence, he screams to Clarence for help: "Please! I want to live again!"

Suddenly the wind dies down and a gentle snow begins to fall. Bert pulls up in his police car, and life is back to normal. Bert knows him, his lip is bleeding again and, yes, Zuzu's petals are back in his pocket. George races through town with unbridled enthusiasm, joyfully shouting to the people and the buildings he sees—to Potter, to the Building and Loan, to the movie theater.

With his usual eye for detail, Capra has an appropriately sentimental movie playing at the theater—Leo McCarey's *The Bells of St. Mary's* (1945), another film that dealt with the basic goodness of the human spirit. It featured Henry Travers in the role of a gruff old man who has a miraculous change of heart and donated money to the church.

Left: Having discovered that he really did have a wonderful life, George is reunited with his family. Though critics may find the emotional conclusion of *It's a Wonderful Life* overly maudlin and loaded with "Capra-corn," many viewers finds it brings tears to the eyes and a lump to the throat—and that was Capra's goal. One of the great directors of Hollywood's Golden Age, Capra and his colleagues had, in Capra's word, the ability to "take an audience by the scruff of the neck and make it shriek with laughter, weep with sorrow, or shake with terror." Part of the secret of Capra's success was that he always had the audience rooting for the underdog, and when George triumphs the audience shares in his victory.

Below: A promotional still highlighting the love story between the two stars. Like George's mother, the audience knows right from the start that George and Mary were made for each other.

In an emotional denouement, the townspeople rally around George in his hour of need. They are all there. Bert, Ernie, Anne the cook, Mr. Martini, Mr. Gower, all the people who jammed the Building and Loan on the day of the bank run. Every single person whose life has been touched by George Bailey crowds into the Bailey home, bringing with them the private reserves of cash they had squirreled away. The only person not among them is Potter. Through it all, George wears a look of disbelief; silently saying the name of each person, relieved—but still slightly incredulous—that everything is back to normal.

Harry proposes a toast to "my big brother, George—the richest man in town." And George is the richest man in town, though his riches are not measured in Potter's terms, but in Clarence's. Buried among the dollar bills is Clarence's copy of *Tom Sawyer* with the words: "Dear George, remember no man is a failure who has friends."

Frank Capra instilled his films with a steadfast belief in the value of friendship and love. His films also expressed love of God and country, but the tone was never preachy; rather it conveyed patriotism and religion in a subtle yet moving way. *It's a Wonderful Life* opens with the townspeople praying, and the original script called for the movie to end with George falling to his knees reciting *The Lord's Prayer.* Wisely, Capra recognized that an overtly religious conclusion would not have the emotional impact of George's friends rushing to his side.

In the movie's final—and perhaps most famous—scene, a bell rings and little Zuzu turns to George and utters the immortal line, "Look Daddy—teacher says every time a bell rings an angel gets his wings." To which George responds, "Atta boy, Clarence."

Though *It's a Wonderful Life* garnered Academy Award nominations for Best Actor, Best Director, and Best Picture, it failed to reap financial rewards at the box office. Although it did moderately well, the Capraesque sentiments that had boosted the spirits of Depression-era audiences seemed outdated to a world that had just witnessed the dawning of a nuclear age. Capra, however, had the last word. *It's a Wonderful Life* was resurrected from oblivion when television stations were looking for cheap Christmas entertainment. By the time of Capra's death in 1991, *It's a Wonderful Life* had become a yuletide tradition, as much a part of Christmas as Santa Claus and his reindeer.

Right: Frank Capra and Jimmy Stewart discuss a scene during the filming of *It's a Wonderful Life.* Capra once said that a director's "best tools are his actors....The story is told through the actors. The audiences you make these pictures for equate with the actors, and not with the camera. When they notice the machinery, your story is out the window. The trick is not to let them notice the machinery. Notice only human beings playing a story up there."

Below: For generations to come, Donna Reed and Jimmy Stewart will entertain movie lovers in the heartwarming tale of George Bailey—a man who discovers it truly is a wonderful life!

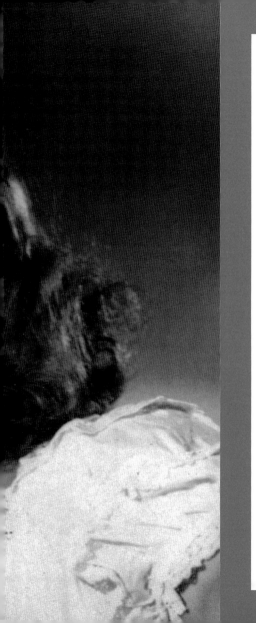

Left: RKO promoted *It's a Wonderful Life* in a number of ways. First, it was a Frank Capra film, and the studio was counting on the Capra name to draw people into the movie houses. Second, to coincide with its December release, the holiday theme was advertised. Finally, the film was touted as a love story. This still of Donna Reed and Jimmy Stewart was one of many taken by RKO's publicity department to create the image of a happy, loving relationship between George and Mary.

Below: As one of Hollywood's favorite leading men, Jimmy Stewart was honored with a star on Hollywood Boulevard.

Index

Acknowledgments

All photos courtesy of American Graphic Systems with the following exceptions:
Ruth DeJauregui: 111
Wisconsin Center for Film & Theater Research: 16-17, 18-19, 26-27, 36-37, 42-43, 54-55, 56-57, 72-73, 98-99